NEMESAI

NEMESAI

John Urbancik

Brian Keene

For Sabine and the Rose Fairy,
and for Starfire and the Forest Fairy

ACKNOWLEDGMENTS

The authors would like to thank all the usual and unusual suspects.

NEMESAI

PART ONE

THE RED DREAMS

1

The world shared the same dream.

Over a few weeks, half of everyone on the planet reported dreaming about it. The phenomenon was not just limited to human. Animals exhibited bizarre behavior—frantically searching for high ground or low ground or shelter or open space, anything or anywhere to protect themselves from what they glimpsed when asleep.

The dream was mostly red. Not blood-red, not wine-red, but some shockingly brilliant never-before-seen shade of red splashed among scenes as deep and dark as humanity had ever imagined and slashes of steel-hued silver mimicking vicious blades. The red stood out starkly against that severe background.

It was a nasty, terrifying dream, so people did what they always do when confronted with such a thing. They packed the bars, emptied their pharmacies of sleeping aids, and watched a lot of late-night television and online videos. In parts of the world without easy access to those sorts of escapes, they gathered at campfires, roasting meats until the morning, and told each other stories and sang and danced and anything else to delay that dreaded sleep.

Stock markets trembled and buckled. Crime skyrocketed. Governments already on the brink of war danced much closer along that edge. But everyone agreed in private that the rise in violence and destruction and death was just a preamble. If the world was a musical, then the current global situation was the overture, suggesting the recurring themes to follow. And such things were indeed coming. People felt it in their marrow, in their hearts, and most especially in the dreams that eventually invaded their waking minds.

Doomsayers rejoiced. They posted on internet forums and obscure social media pages and celebrated the fact they were right—the end of the world was finally happening. They couldn't reach a consensus on what form it would take, but all of them agreed this time, it was real.

In some places, scientists tackled questions. So did philosophers, military strategists, and random self-appointed pseudo-journalists.

But they were the exceptions. Most people didn't talk publicly about the red dreams. They might mention it in private, in hushed conversations with a loved one or trusted friend. But they didn't discuss it with anyone else. Many feared speaking about the dreams would bring those night terrors into their waking life.

That happened anyway.

2

A ten-year old girl in Xi'an, China first witnessed the dream made flesh.

She sat alone outside the city wall, facing east to watch the sunrise. The reds of the dawn were far more understandable than the reds of her dreams—and much more pleasant.

The city was quiet, and the stillness disturbed her. There were no horns honking or motors thrumming. Xi'an's inhabitants—the few who still went about their daily business—seemed listless, almost lifeless. The forests beyond the city were also silent. There was no birdsong or wind, as if an unnatural stillness had coated the world like an oil slick, clinging to everything.

Dawn, perhaps, was the last bit of nature she could recognize. That was why she sat there, anxiously awaiting it. Everything was better in daylight.

But something preceded the sun. She heard it and felt it long before she saw it. The ground shook, as if from some far-off artillery strike. The treetops of the forest swayed, but no wind moved them. The silence was broken by the sound of snapping trunks and splintering wood. One by one, the trees toppled, and something terrible emerged from the forest. The thing was impossibly large, riding astride an equally massive bestial, red mount.

At first, she thought the rider was a giant man. It was *like* a man, having two legs and two arms, a head, and a face—a horrible face, a countenance radiating terror—a burning, red face, the red of her nightmares, the red that came before the end of everything. It was a creature unlike anything the girl had seen in any story, movie, or game. Its mount—as unlike a horse as the rider was unlike a man—snorted with a noise like phlegmatic thunder. As she gaped in shock, it pawed at the ground with massive hooves, uprooting rocks and digging deep furrows in the earth. The ragged trenches reminded the girl of wounds.

The rider carried long, jagged weapons in both hands. The weapons, too, were unlike anything she had ever seen before, a fiendish combination of swords and spears and sawblades.

The monstrosity rode up to the city wall and struck, lashing out. The wall crumbled like paper.

Both the rider and its mount howled in unison. The sound boomed across the landscape.

The cries were soon joined by the screams of the city's populace.

The giant cut a path of destruction through Xi'an, never wavering, pausing only long enough to bring down the buildings in its way and slaughter those who weren't smart enough to flee. Thousands died attempting to escape. Not everyone in Xi'an died by the attacker's hand. Some were crushed beneath the wreckage or burned alive in the fires left in its wake or perished from heart attacks and seizures brought on by fear and shock.

Later, after the creature and its monstrous mount had disappeared, when plumes of smoke still rose from the ruins and vultures circled, waiting for the fires to cool, a group of first responders found the girl on the outskirts of the city. Her ears and eyes were bleeding, and she had no tears left to cry.

3

The girl told her story once, to the rescuers who found her, and then never spoke again. She was transported to a makeshift triage area, before being transported to a hospital. After a dose of sedatives, the little girl slept peacefully for the first time in weeks.

The red of her dreams was a comfort in comparison to the nightmare made real.

4

The city of Zhengzhou was the next to fall, less than twenty-four hours after the destruction in Xi'an.

The media quickly dubbed the creature Nemesai: the ultimate nemesis of man.

Three days later, another such devil devastated a series of small villages and rustic farming communities.

North and South Korea, Japan, and most Asian nations put themselves on alert, and increased security around their borders.

The Chinese military finally mustered an organized response outside Shanghai. Frightened but steadfast soldiers stood their ground as one of the giant Nemesai rode toward the city. Many of the soldiers had a picture of the girl from Xi'an—an image taken from social media—pinned to their helmets or uniforms. When the Nemesai halted, the order to attack was given—and they engaged. Smoke from the battle enshrouded half the city. They fired guns first, then missiles and laser-guided advanced weaponry. Tons of lead rained down. Megatons of explosives rocked the earth as they unleashed hell on the single Nemesai and its demonic mount.

For the next six hours, the Nemesai and its mount stood their ground, accepting everything the Chinese army threw at them—artillery, tanks, and ground troops. Both creatures took deep inhalations of the smoke and dust and dirt in the air, but remained in place as the ground trembled and cratered all around them. The Nemesai moved only to raise its head, watching impassively as fighter jets and bombers unloaded on it to no avail.

Finally, there was a lull in the attack, and the creature spurred its ride forward.

Then it proceeded to dismantle Shanghai and almost every living thing that dwelled there.

Except the soldiers.

It deliberately left the soldiers alive.

They were still crying out as it rode away.

5

"These dreams are warnings," an old man said to his granddaughter. "From the Ancestors."

It was why he had packed their cart and rode out of Shanghai three days earlier, escaping the devastation.

"I don't like them," the eight-year-old said.

"You're not supposed to," the grandfather replied. "Our Ancestors faced this day once before, many generations before you were born."

"And before you were born?"

He nodded. "Oh, yes."

The girl giggled. "That's a long time ago."

"Longer ago than anyone now remembers. It happened before even China herself was born."

"There has always been a China," the girl said, because she knew this as an absolute truth. "The land didn't just suddenly get born one day. It doesn't work that way."

"You're right, of course," the grandfather said. "But this land wasn't always called China. Once upon a time, a great many warring states divided our land. And before Ying Zhèng could unite us, he had to face our truest enemies."

"No," the girl said. Again, she was proud of what she knew. "It was Qin Shi Haungdi who united China."

"Yes," the grandfather agreed. "But before he became known as the Son of Heaven, he led a nation, and an army. He was king of Qin, little one. In fact, he had that title since he was almost your age."

"Did he save us?" the girl asked.

"Yes, according to the legends."

"Will he come back and save us again?"

For this, the grandfather had no answer. He guided their cart forward, hoping when they stopped for the night, and he went to sleep next to his granddaughter, they both would see a color other than red.

6

Atiya Destine dealt with the red dreams by sleeping. She did so lucidly, aware the entire time she was dreaming, and thus, able to control her environment to some extent. She moved around in the dreams each night, seeking answers, solving riddles, poking and prodding into places her waking self was reluctant to go. She went anyhow, because these were only dreams. She'd faced far more terrifying things in real life.

Despite her best efforts, she didn't learn much.

Regardless, she wasn't about to let these dreams destroy her life. Living required too much effort. Understanding required even more. Atiya had spent her entire life seeking in the farthest, deepest, strangest corners of the Earth, discovering whatever new thing she could find, and rediscovering old things that had been forgotten. Sometimes she sold those old things for money. Sometimes she sold herself as a guide to places others would never find on their own. In her time, she'd been sought after by most of the world's biggest private security firms and military companies, courted by corporations like Globe and Alpinus Biofutures, and even wooed by secretive, esoteric orders from Black Lodge to the Order of the White Raven. But while Atiya would freelance for them on occasion, she never joined, turning down every offer of membership or initiation, no matter how financially lucrative or secure.

The only people she swore allegiance to were her team. They showed her loyalty, and that was worth more than any financial remuneration. They were mercenaries and adventurers, a core of six with support from a dozen more. With Atiya as their leader, they'd recovered stolen jewels, precious artifacts, and historic artwork. They'd tracked kidnappers and battled human traffickers, drug cartels, organized criminals and supernatural occultists. Via an unfortunate twist of events, they searched for, found, and lost a relic so rare the Vatican almost sent a team to take them down. Twice.

Atiya wasn't merely an adventurer, nor an archeologist, nor a historian, nor a soldier. She was all of those things. She wasn't simply a girl or a woman, either; that would never do. She was Atiya Destine, and she was everything she wanted to be. Nothing more, and nothing less.

She suffered through the red dreams because she wanted to find a way to end them.

It had nothing to do with saving the world. She sought only a good night's sleep. And since she rarely remembered her dreams after waking, she knew the only solution in vanquishing them was would have to happen in her sleep.

When she woke, Atiya didn't know if she had succeeded. She only knew she'd slept longer than the night before. She stirred, rolled over, and stared, blurry-eyed, at the red numbers on her digital alarm clock.

But they were the only red she saw.

"Progress," she muttered.

She turned on the news and saw images from her dreams brought to life: fire on the streets of some Chinese city, reports of at least two separate creatures. A satellite image showed one, overly blurred, a red scar on the face of the earth, cutting new roads through a forest as it advanced relentlessly on some other, unprotectable village hurriedly being evacuated.

"Nothing seems to hurt them," the breathless

reporter was saying. "Nothing slows them down. It's like they're not human."

"They're not," Atiya told the television as she switched the channel. "Moron. Nothing about them looks human."

"No official tally yet," another reporter said, "but officials told us, on condition of anonymity, the dead number in the tens of thousands, and there are at least twice as many wounded. Hospitals are overflowing, temporary triage centers have been set up across the region, and a local skating rink has been turned into a makeshift morgue."

Yawning, Atiya changed the channel yet again. This news network featured an anchor sitting behind a fancy ultra-modern chrome and glass desk, interviewing a pundit on a split screen.

"What if this is just the first wave?" the pundit asked. "What if there are more and they begin showing up elsewhere in the world? The President and his cabinet don't seem prepared to—"

Atiya turned off the television, having learned everything she needed to. The red dreams weren't just dreams anymore. They were real. Asking if the Nemesai were a part of a first wave was ridiculous. More likely, they were scouts on a reconnaissance mission, testing defenses and offensive capabilities.

Today was the first day the news hadn't shown footage of the ruins of Shanghai. Even so, she thought of Stefan anyway.

Using an encrypted phone, Atiya sent a text message to the members of her team. Then she took a long shower, enjoying the luxuriant feeling of the hot water on her skin. Emerging, she wiped steam from the mirror with her towel, stared unblinking at her expression for several minutes, and then brushed her teeth. After getting dressed, she checked the phone. There were two replies, from Jude and Johnson, respectively. The other four team members had yet to respond. Jude didn't mention Stefan by name, but his text mentioned a potential new recruit. Atiya frowned.

She held the phone in her hand, staring at it. Then, she lay down on the couch and took another nap, still hoping to find more answers in her sleep.

She suspected they'd need those answers more than ever in the days ahead.

PART TWO

MAUSOLEUM

1

The pyramid-shaped necropolis, which was over two thousand years old and pre-dated the Western Christ, stood not far from Xi'an, forgotten amidst the chaos. Big as a small city, pearl stars in its ceiling were said to map the night sky. At one point in history, traps in its walls had been set with crossbows, and it was sealed by molten copper. Eight thousand giant terracotta soldiers had once guarded the massive burial mound. The site, closed to the public for years due to fears of quicksilver contamination, was guarded around the clock to prevent trespassers. Most of the structure was located underground. Its surface was covered with trees and dirt and rocks.

Atiya and her team set up camp out of sight of the burial mound. They were close enough to Xi'an to smell the aftermath of the devastation. Each time the wind shifted, it brought with it the stench of death and decay. Flocks of carrion birds darkened the sky overhead, rushing to the grisly buffet.

Crossing into China had been simple enough. Jude had already been inside the country. The others encountered no problems. Security around the border was weakened given the fact that the enemy was striking at the country's heart. In the days since Atiya had assembled her team, the Nemesai had moved beyond China, laying waste to Kolkata, Tokyo, and more. Their paths of destruction were neither symmetrical nor straight, but Jude had been tracking them.

"They're estimating between three and twenty dead now," he told Atiya. "That's millions."

Atiya sighed. "They've barely begun. These are still early days."

"Yeah…"

"Any idea where they're going next?"

Jude handled communications, satellites, computers, and all of the other technological stuff Atiya pretended not to care about. The truth was, she was almost as tech-savvy as Jude, just usually busy dealing with other matters. They'd met back in Berlin, when people still remembered what it was like before the wall had come down, before their little group officially formed. He was as close to a brother as Atiya knew.

"I'm doing my best." He shrugged. "But no. At least we know they're not coming here, right?"

"Check again," she told him. "You might be surprised."

2

In addition to Atiya and Jude, the rest of the team bustled around the campsite.

Christine was their explosives and demolition expert. She'd once disarmed a bomb meant to take down the London Tower back in 2011, but of course, no one ever heard about it because she'd done her job so well.

Keith embodied pure fury with firepower. Something had happened to him once, something he never talked about. Atiya had spent months trying to find out, but there were no records. Whatever it had been, the event had scarred him, made him—not evil, not malicious, but reckless and angry and, above all else, laser focused. Keith was like the guns he favored. All he needed was someone to aim him in the direction of whatever needed shot.

Johnson served as their diplomat. He was best at making and keeping connections, greasing what needed to be greased, crossing palms, and arranging for whatever they needed. He'd had politicians for parents—ambassadors or something—who had died in South Africa when he was a teenager. Johnson had a history of womanizing. He could sometimes be arrogant and aggressive. Atiya was certain one day that combination would get him killed. She didn't want to be there for that, but it seemed inevitable.

The newest addition to the team called herself Jane, but that wasn't her real name. None of them knew her real name. She was a last-minute replacement for Stefan, their resident linguist. Jane was Chinese, and thus far had spoken no English, but Atiya knew that was a ruse. For this mission, she was meant to be their guide, their translator, and ultimately, their expert on Chinese history and culture and legend. She'd been an academic of some sort, according to Jude, who had rescued her from the rubble of Shanghai after the Nemesai attacked the city. Atiya was hesitant to take her on, but Jude made a convincing argument, speaking to the younger woman's desire for the same things they wanted—stopping the Nemesai. Jane kept to herself, and largely held her tongue, probably still in shock.

The team was like a jigsaw puzzle. Atiya had spent years carefully putting the pieces together. Stefan was a missing piece, glaring in his absence when viewing the puzzle as a whole. Jane was a replacement piece, and it remained to be seen how well she would fit.

3

Their camp had been made. They were seated in a circle, except for Jane, who sat slightly behind Jude, knees drawn up against her chest, arms wrapped around her legs. They had no fire, no food cooking, no music — nothing that would indicate their presence in the darkness beneath the trees.

"Why here?" Johnson asked.

"If you mean, why do I think it's here," Atiya replied, "I'll get to that, in time. But if you mean, why do I think the Nemesai originated from here, I have a hunch. But I'm not an expert, so…"

"Yeah?" Johnson's tone was impatient.

Atiya nodded toward Jane. "Maybe she'll be able to tell us that. Eventually. If we find anything useful."

Jane hugged her knees more tightly. She'd said nothing, but her eyes never left Atiya.

"Somebody give me a flashlight," Atiya said.

Christine pulled a small flashlight, shaped like a cigarette lighter, from her gear, and handed it over. Atiya thanked her, and then spread a cloth map on the ground between them. Then she turned on the light, careful to keep the thin beam pointed at the map.

"The first attack was at Xi'an. The second attack happened in Zhengzhou. We're basically between those two locations now. I'm guessing they emerged from here and then fanned out across the land."

"You're guessing?" Johnson asked.

Atiya raised her eyebrows. "Is there a problem?"

Johnson grinned. "Not at all. Your guesses are better than the average genius's facts. I'm just seeking clarification, intel-wise. What about the site itself?"

Atiya looked to Christine. "First, we have to get in."

"Are there sensors? Cameras?"

"Plenty," Atiya said, "but no mines or barbed wire or things like that."

"I thought this was going to be difficult."

"Don't get cocky, Christine. I want you and Keith to do reconnaissance. Survey the mound. Find the best point of entry and determine if there's any military or security to deal with."

"Surely they're all deployed to deal with the Nemesai," Johnson said.

"Possibly," Atiya said, "but it's reasonable to expect a skeleton crew has been left behind to guard it. Remember, we're not here by invitation."

Jane rocked gently back and forth and closed her eyes. Atiya watched her for a moment, and then turned back to Johnson. "If there are guards stationed, you'll arrange for us to get in, yes?"

He nodded. "Of course."

"Okay, then you go along with Christine and Keith, but hang back unless needed. Got it?"

All three nodded in confirmation, and then departed the campsite, slipping quietly into the darkness, leaving Jude, Atiya and Jane.

"You were right," Jude said, looking up from his laptop computer. "I know how much you like hearing me say that."

"About what?"

"The Nemesai. They've turned around. Taking different routes back to this location. Doing whatever damage they can along the way."

Atiya sighed. "I suspected as much."

"They're scouts, aren't they?"

She nodded. "Returning to their army."

Jude snorted. "They don't need an army. Look how much devastation they've caused on their own, just the two of them."

"Imagine how much a full force of them could do." She settled back but found herself unable to relax. Her spine felt like it was composed of tight knots.

"*Bu*," Jane whispered, rocking back and forth.

After a moment, Jude said, "I believe Stefan is still alive."

"If that's so," Atiya said, "then why didn't you bring him with you from Shanghai rather than her?"

"Because I couldn't find him. But that doesn't mean he's dead."

Atiya didn't want to think about Stefan. He was part of their core—confidante, friend, lover. There wasn't much room for any of those things in Atiya's life, but he served as all three, and she alternately hated and loved him for it. Right now, she hated him—because of the uncertainty of his fate. He and Jude had been in Shanghai when the Nemesai arrived. Both men had lived through the red dreams, survived the massacre, and crawled through the blood of thousands to escape. Jude said Stefan had saved people along the way, and they'd lost track of each other. Could it be possible he was still alive, with all that happened? With all that was still happening?

"He'll come," Jude said. "Give him time."

"I don't care."

"Of course you don't." Jude grinned. "But he'll be here, nonetheless. He's probably on his way now, on the back of a donkey or something."

"After what he's seen," Atiya said, "he probably couldn't stand it."

"Jane saw it, too," Jude replied, "and she's here."

Jane's eyes shifted from Jude to Atiya. She scooted a few inches back, but still said nothing.

Atiya wanted to lash out at the younger woman, punish her for being here instead of Stefan. She shuddered, holding back tears.

"He's your knight," Jude whispered.

Atiya hardened her glare. "Drop it."

"Dropped."

"I think it's nice," Jane said in perfect, if clipped, English. "I wish I had someone to feel about that way."

Jude gaped. "You…speak English?"

Jane nodded.

"Wow…well, I guess that will make translating easier. I thought I'd have to speak for you. Why didn't you tell me before?"

"You I trusted. I had to…see about the others."

Atiya ignored the exchange. "How much time do we have before the Nemesai arrive back here?"

Jude stared at his screen for a moment, then folded it shut. "Two days? Four at the most. Depends on how often they stop to destroy things on the way back."

Atiya nodded. Two to four days. She needed to come up with a plan before then—and before her team figured out she didn't have one.

4

Christine followed Keith toward the perimeter. Johnson had ignored Atiya's orders and gone his own way, having a different intention. Christine was glad for that. She didn't like him, had never liked him, and barely trusted him. The things that made him so good at his job also made him the worst kind of person.

Christine liked people, generally.

For instance, she liked Keith. They'd transitioned from straight-forward fucking to something like making love.

Keith knew the difference. Johnson would never understand.

But on the way to the burial mound, she and Keith were all business. Both carried their weapons at the ready, and proceeded with military precision, not breaking protocol for even a loving glance or quick flirtation.

Keith halted, motioning at the ground. Christine looked where he pointed, and eventually saw the outline of a pressure plate beneath the soil. Not a mine. It was some kind of sensor, most likely triggering a silent alarm if something stepped on it. They moved stealthily around it.

"Fucking Johnson," Keith whispered. "Hope he doesn't set one of those off."

"He works better alone," Christine said. "Always has. He says the rest of us just throw him off. We're a distraction."

"Throw him off? His superpower is *talking*. Johnson's a con man, plain and simple."

"He is, but he's also good at what he does. Remember the Order of the White Raven?"

Keith nodded.

"He got us out of that fiasco," Christine said. "Or the time he charmed that pharmaceutical magnate's widow into giving us the *Book of Lost Fates*?"

"Too bad he couldn't do the same for John Dee's copy of the *Daemonolateria*. We all nearly got killed."

"Johnson didn't know at the time it was a fake. None of us did."

Keith grunted. "I guess you're right. Credit where it's due, I haven't forgotten about the art dealer hopped up on that synthetic opioid...what was it called?"

"Scarlet."

"Yeah, that's it. That guy would have killed you if Johnson hadn't talked him down. But I still don't like him."

They fell silent again, and carefully worked their way around a group of security cameras mounted to the trees.

"Ever think this might be our last game?" Keith whispered.

He always called each mission a game. For him, it had all started as a game. He'd been a child on a soccer field, one child amongst many, when the soldiers came. He'd never talked about it with anyone other than Christine. He'd told her about the twelve-year-old girl begging for her life, and the solider offering it to her for such a small price. He'd seen them in the alley, through the smoke and the dust. The girl had cried so very badly. Keith, all of ten years old at the time, and barely understood what was happening, what the blood on the girl's bare thighs meant. But he'd understood what was happening when, after the invader was finished with her, he put his pistol to the back of the girl's neck—while she was still on hands and knees—and blew her brains out.

And Keith understood what he'd done to the soldier while the man was attempting to pull up his pants. Keith knew what he'd done to the man—first with a brick, and then with his hands—and finally his teeth.

The memory made Christine shudder, even though it wasn't hers.

"Then we play to win," Christine said.

Before he could respond, they stopped, having reached the mound. Christine had expected some sort of security fence around it, at the very least. There wouldn't be a historical marker or anything for tourists, but surely there would be something to mark its location. In reality, the site wasn't much more than a mountain.

"Come on," she whispered, creeping forward. "Let's go play to win."

Keith shifted his rifle in his hands. "I think the best we can hope for, Chris, is a stalemate.

5

It was just before midnight when Christine and Keith returned.

"Where's Johnson?" Atiya asked.

"He's off doing his own thing," Christine replied. "Sorry."

Atiya sighed, exasperated. "Sit-rep?"

"No live security," Keith reported, sounding disappointed. "No personnel whatsoever, other than the dead. Looks like the Nemesai mowed them down first, before launching the attack on Xi'an."

"We located a readymade entry point," Christine said. "A huge hole. It slips under the copper, and it's already been opened."

"That's how the Nemesai got out," Atiya said.

"Looks that way," Christine agreed. "Dirt and debris on the outside. It wasn't blown out, though. Dug by hand is my guess."

"So…" Atiya steepled her fingers together. "They emerge from the burial mound, kill the forces guarding it, then head out on their scouting expedition, laying siege to Xi'an and elsewhere in the process."

"Looks like you were right all along," Jude said.

Atiya nodded. "And now they're on their way back here."

Christina's eyes widened. "Excuse me, *what?*"

"Jude says we've got two to four days before they arrive."

"Shit," Keith muttered. "I'm going to need more guns."

"Guns are useless against those things." Stifling a

groan, Atiya rose to her feet. "We need to get moving. We have a deadline now."

"Shouldn't we wait for Johnson?" Jude asked, rising to his feet, as well.

"No time," Atiya said, grabbing her gear. "We'll catch him on the way."

Keith stood still. "You knew this was a possibility, didn't you?"

Atiya paused. She looked at her team, one-by-one. She slumped her shoulders, sighing.

"I suspected. I don't know anything more about the Nemesai than the rest of you do. Remember, that's the entire point. We're here to find out everything we can about them."

"So…" Christine hesitated. "Maybe it's time you told us who is funding this mission?"

"We don't have a benefactor this time," Atiya admitted. "No government, no private individual with a taste for vengeance, no law enforcement agency reaching beyond their reach. I'm bankrolling it myself. Don't worry. You'll all get paid."

"I'm not worried about getting paid," Christine countered. "I'm worried about the fact that you didn't level with us from the start. That's not like you, Atiya."

"I know. It's not. I…haven't been myself. I don't think anyone has. Not since the dreams started. For what it's worth, I'm sorry."

"Why not just inform the Chinese government of our intentions?" Jude asked. "They might have given us assistance."

"We've always operated beneath the radar."

"But still…"

"Look," Atiya said, "it's better this way. There was no need to attract attention. If we succeed, then we can continue to operate in anonymity. If we fail, then at least we won't have given the world any false hope."

Jude, Christine, and Keith glanced at each other. Jane stared at the ground. Atiya turned away from them and started off, knowing they would follow.

6

They found Johnson standing outside the burial mound, in view of the opening Christine and Keith had found.

"There's no one here," Johnson said.

"Yeah," Keith said, "we figured that out already. Where the fuck have you been?"

"Double checking you."

"Fuck you."

Atiya interrupted the two men. "Seriously, Johnson. Where were you?"

"I thought there might be refugees from Xi'an making their way through here, so I checked for that."

"And were there?"

He shook his head. "The roads and forests are empty. And not just of people. There's no wildlife. Even the birds are gone. This place feels wrong."

The others nodded in agreement.

Johnson nodded at the hole. "I think they came out through there. You were right, Atiya. This is their point of origin."

"And this is where they're coming back to," Jude said.

Johnson's eyes grew wide. "Excuse me?"

While the others filled him in, Atiya stared at the hole. It wasn't in the burial mound itself, but beside its base. The mound was almost a pyramid, and huge. Miles across above ground, and probably larger underground.

Keith opened his oversized backpack and pulled out six canary-yellow hazardous material suits with built in gas masks.

"This thing will be a lot lighter now," he said as he passed them out. "Sometimes I think I'm just a pack-mule."

"Well, you are a bit of a jackass," Jude teased.

"Better make sure I don't poke a hole in your suit."

As Atiya slipped into hers, she saw Christine helping Jane. The new recruit stared at the apparatus dubiously.

Christine turned to Jude. "Can you explain to her we're expecting mercury, or possibly other bio-agents?"

"No need," he replied. "As it turns out, Jane speaks English."

Jane smile sheepishly and nodded.

"Oh." Christine's grinned in return. "Okay, then make sure you keep this on at all times. Those vapors will make you mad as a hatter. That's what happened to Jude."

"Hey!" He chuckled.

Jane tapped the circular lenses on her gas mask. "What are these?"

"Night vision and ultraviolet spectrum lenses," Christine explained. "There's also a flashlight built into each one. Here, I'll show you how to turn it on."

"I have never seen suits like these before."

"These are high tech," Atiya told her. "Each one has an oxygen generator and a carbon dioxide scrubber, just like they use in space and under the sea. Your air supply can last up to eight hours, under normal physical exertion. When it's running low, they'll beep. Then it's as simple as changing the cartridge in it. There are radios inside each suit, so we'll be able to hear one another easily enough. They have a battery life of twenty-four hours. You'll probably get hot inside this thing, but again, don't take it off. Mercury can be absorbed through the skin and your mucous membranes. We need to limit exposure as much as possible."

"Radio check," Jude said.

Each one pressed a button on their wrist and spoke in turn, and he verified the microphone in each suit was working.

When they were ready, the group fell silent and approached the hole. Keith took point, moving ahead of the rest of them. They followed single file, with Atiya next, then Christine, Jane, and Jude. Johnson brought up the rear. Keith brought them to a halt at the recently made crack in the earth.

"It looks stable," he whispered.

Atiya nodded. "Let's go."

The night-vision turned everything into green blobs and silhouettes, and their breath sounded distorted. Dust and dirt and sand dribbled on them as they climbed through the hole. The ground sloped downwards, and inward, toward the heart of the underground necropolis.

"Quicksilver rivers and pearl stars in the ceiling," Jude muttered. "That's what they say, at least."

"Quiet," Atiya warned. "We'll switch from night-vision to flashlight beams when we know it's safe. Single file, and watch your step...and each other's backs."

They proceeded in silence, heading deeper into the earth.

7

Atiya found things. It was her joy. Her passion. Her purpose. Everything else was extraneous. Since she'd stumbled into the catacombs under Paris at the age of twelve, she'd spent most her life crawling through the dark and making discoveries.

Her father had been a spy, and her mother a defense analysist. Growing up, Atiya had been trained in firearms from the age of six. Her parents had reasoned that, with guns in the household, it was better to teach her how to use them safely than suffer an accident. Atiya learned how to throw a kick around the same time she learned to run.

She first took another person's life at age nine.

Her father had met someone in the depths of a car park, but their meeting had been spoiled by a trio of masked men. She didn't know details, not then and not ever, but she knew the guys with the guns wanted to kill her dad and his friend. But they didn't know about her in the car, in the shadows. Pulse pounding in her ears and throat, so scared she nearly peed her pants, she slipped a 9mm out from under the seat.

It was a clean shot through the side of the head. The assailant lingered a moment, looking surprised. Then he dropped. Her father pulled his weapon and shot the other two in quick succession. She remembered that afterward, her father had tried to comfort her, but she couldn't hear him because her ears still rang from the gunshots.

Atiya's first big find had been a pyramid. It was nothing spectacular, like those in Giza or Central America. In fact, this particular pyramid was located in

Central America, and it had already been discovered many times before. It was a few days before her eighteenth birthday, and she had traveled there to celebrate. When the opportunity presented itself, she had snuck away from the guided tour group and gone off to explore on her own. Ultimately, she found a burial chamber previously unknown to archeologists or generations of grave robbers.

Now, as they made their way into the interior of the burial mound of the first emperor of China, Atiya took comfort in the fact that while it was known, no human being had been inside in over two centuries. No one knew what was there, waiting to be found.

For Atiya, it should have been a moment of pure ecstasy.

Instead, the further they descended, all she felt was an increasing sense of dread.

8

The girl and her grandfather had indeed escaped Shanghai, but their safety was relative. No place in China — or indeed the world — was safe now. Even sleep wasn't an escape, given the red dreams humanity shared.

The two took shelter in a small farming village, where a kind Samaritan had allowed them to stay in a barn.

One night, the girl asked her grandfather how he knew about the red dreams.

"My grandfather," he said, "who learned from our ancestors. Would you like to know more?"

She nodded eagerly.

"Imagine our lives as a blanket," her grandfather said. "Some histories and legends weave their way through the generations the way you weave thread on a loom. They become part of the fabric of our past and identity. But other histories and legends are forgotten, and end up lost. Sometimes, a few threads manage to get passed down as familial lore, but those threads are frayed and weak. Do you understand, little one?"

"Yes."

"We are descended from Li Si."

"Who was that?"

"Ying Zhèng's chancellor while he was king of Qin, through his short reign as first emperor, and even longer than that. These particular stories had never been written down by our ancestors, and never shared with outsiders — not just foreigners, but anyone from outside our family. And you must promise to do the same."

"I will."

"Our truest enemies were imprisoned by the ancestors of our ancestors. Locked away by magic."

"My teacher says there is no magic."

"Then you teacher leads a very sad life. Magic exists. It is merely science we can't yet explain. That's what they used to imprison our enemies—what they now call the Nemesai. But they eventually found a way out of the earth's core, and they rose up to destroy the king and all of his subjects and all his friends and all his enemies."

"Did they have the red dreams then, too?"

"The red dreams, no. But they had a warning. They read the oracle bones."

9

Having switched from night-vision to flashlights, Atiya's group stood gaping in astonishment. Mercury rivers ran through what seemed to be a hugely oversized map of China. Aging footbridges crossed the flows. Pearls dotted the massive copper dome over their heads. Full-sized huts had been built alongside the riverbanks. Some of the hut walls were etched with lines of Chinese calligraphy. More symbols, drawn in pits of sand, had been untouched for more than two thousand years. There were tapestries and golden carvings, running fountains of quicksilver, and lines of what had once been terracotta warriors.

Once been—because every single warrior had been smashed.

Shards were scattered haphazardly. Bronze weapons lay where they'd fallen, swords and spears and other blades, along with bows and arrows. Some were broken, but many seemed untouched.

The terracotta warriors, on the other hand, had been obliterated beyond repair.

Atiya pointed at the calligraphy, and then turned to Jane. "Start looking for anything that mentions the Nemesai. Johnson, you go with her. And be careful. We don't know how stable those structures are."

Jane stared at her, without moving. "I...what if there's something down here with us?"

"You told Jude you wanted to help," Atiya said. "Now's the time to start helping."

Jane tilted her head to the side.

Atiya held her anger. "It'll be okay." She hated how muffled and tinny her voice sounded through the suit.

Jane bowed her head, and then set off, following Johnson. He tentatively stepped onto one of the bridges. Surprisingly, it held his weight easily.

"They don't make them like that anymore," Keith muttered.

They watched as Jane also crossed the footbridge without incident.

"The rest of you," Atiya said, pointing in another direction, "let's check the perimeter. Keith and Christine, you go that way. Jude and I will head in this direction. We'll meet back here."

Nodding, Christine and Keith headed off to explore. Jude and Atiya did the same.

The underground complex deepened toward the center, and spanned so far it had its own horizon. Atiya marveled as they walked. The artwork was unlike anything she'd ever seen. The huts were open, with no doors in the doorways and no glass in the windows. All of the buildings she and Jude encountered were empty but sturdy. Remarkably, the wood was free of rot or mold, as were the fabrics used to decorate the outsides.

"The condition of this place," Atiya asked. "Is that because of the mercury? Is it acting as some sort of…preservative?"

"I don't know," Jude admitted. "Maybe we should look into bringing a metallurgist or a chemist onto the team. Or maybe an alchemist. You know they thought of mercury as the first matter from which all other metals were formed. They used it when trying to turn base metals into gold."

"How does that help us now?"

"It doesn't," he admitted. "I'm just making conversation."

"What else do you know about this place?" She gestured with a sweep of her hand.

"Not much. That's why I enlisted Jane. I know the emperor thought the mercury would give him immortality. He had a basin filled with it, and he used to sleep on a floating mattress in the middle of it. Of course, he died of mercury poisoning, but he never gave up his belief in its properties. That's why he buried himself with the mercury rivers—along with the royal treasury."

"I haven't seen any treasury," Atiya said. "And I haven't seen any tomb."

"This whole thing was his tomb."

"No," Atiya said. "This is more than just a tomb."

During their exploration, they found more shards of terracotta warriors, but none still intact. Outside of one structure, three pairs of terracotta legs stood not much higher than their knees. The rest of these warriors were scattered fragments.

"This was done recently," Atiya said. "There's no dust on the broken pieces."

"You think the Nemesai did this before coming out?"

Atiya nodded.

"Why?" Jude asked. "Why take the time to destroy every statue in this place?"

"I hope Jane can answer that, because I'd really like to know."

Jude yawned beneath his mask.

"Am I boring you?" Atiya asked.

"No. Cut me some slack. I've been awake almost thirty-six hours. We all have."

"You should have slept when you had the chance."

"And have more of those red dreams? No thanks."

Eventually, they returned to their starting point,

having found no other entrances. The outer walls were solid, with not even a crack. Christine and Keith reported the same.

"I keep wondering why there wasn't more ecological damage around this site," Christine said. "You would think water run-off from the mercury would have poisoned the ground outside. But nothing can escape this place."

"Something sure did," Jude said.

Christine shrugged. "Yeah, I guess you're right."

"Have any of you noticed there's no life down here?" Jude asked. "No insects or animals. At the very least, we should have seen bats or grubs or millipedes. I suppose the mercury could account for that, but still…"

"I've got a theory about these broken warrior statues," Keith said.

Atiya stifled her surprise. "You do?"

He nodded. "They were practice dummies for the Nemesai. Just like targets on the range."

Before anyone could respond, the radios crackled with static.

"Atiya?" Johnson's voice sounded distorted. "I think you ought to come see this."

She keyed her microphone. "Where are you?"

"Straight into the city's center. We should be easy to find. I think all the roads lead here."

"Copy that," Atiya replied. "We're on our way."

10

The group stood in front of the final resting place of China's first emperor.

The tomb occupied the city's center. It was surrounded by piles of ancient coinage and gold, and pots full of mercury, parchments and weapons, and the shattered remains of more terracotta soldiers.

More interesting was the massive stairway spiraling deeper into the bowels of the earth.

PART THREE

THE OTHER TEAM

1

Stefan's new team consisted of three people—the only three he needed.

As far as Stefan was concerned, the people on Atiya's team were on their own. He wished them no ill will. Well, maybe Johnson. Yeah, Johnson could go fuck himself. But the others were fine individuals. Jude has done his best to save Stefan back in Shanghai, not knowing he still lived. Stefan had wanted the rest of them to think him dead; that would make what he had to do much easier. Perhaps they would mourn him for a brief moment. Perhaps they already had. But their grief would be short and then they'd get back to the job. He would miss them in the same manner.

But now it was time to go back to work.

He cared about Atiya. Felt something for her, of course. They were in love, as much so as either of them was capable, which perhaps wasn't much—but it was something. In this world, you grabbed whatever little something you could, because chances were against another opportunity down the road. Despite that, he needed her to think he was dead, because Atiya's team—and Atiya herself—didn't have what it would take to defeat the Nemesai.

He knew that first hand, after what he'd witnessed in Shanghai.

He'd accepted Atiya's theory that the red dreams and the Nemesai were connected. Obviously. And he agreed they had emerged from the center of the earth. But they were not avenging angels or apocalyptic demons like some desperate people on the internet claimed.

They were just what they were: enemies of humanity, enemies of life, *Nemesai.*

Stefan had seen the creature in Shanghai up close and personal. He'd filled it with every ounce of lead he had on him. He'd tossed grenades at it. When he ran out of both, he'd swung at it in a desperate, seemingly futile attempt. Hitting it was like punching a brick wall, but amazingly, the creature felt the blow. Bullets bounced away like the thing was invulnerable, but Stefan's fist made a miniscule, momentary indention in the skin—the smallest of victories in such a scenario, but there it was. These creatures weren't invincible or invulnerable. You just needed someone with a little more muscle behind their punches. Mike Tyson, maybe. George Foreman. Ali. Frazier. Lennox. De La Hoya. Dempsey. If none of them were immediately available (or alive), you went with what you had.

So, after emerging alive from the wreckage left behind in the Nemesai's wake, Stefan had called on Frankie.

Frankie was a bulldozer. A brick wall with tree trunk legs. An attitude with muscle. His perpetual sneer showed off the spaces of his missing three teeth. His nose was as crooked as a cheap-suited politician, and he always had an appetite for a fight.

Stefan had never seen him lose.

But this was it, the heavyweight championship of the world. There'd be no belt, no title, no referee—and no bell. This would be a balls-out knuckler, with no corner to retreat to between rounds. Despite Frankie's formidable size and skills, Stefan knew it would take more than brawn to defeat their enemy. That was why he had also called in Charlie.

Charlie had the cameras, the wheels, and the computers. He was a mini-Jude, but a freelancer, an outsider, and he only took the job because there were no other jobs to take. Not anymore. In the era of the Nemesai and the red dreams that preceded them, nobody cared about anything anymore. The world was falling apart. Operatives like Frankie and Charlie were needed now more than ever, but there was no one to hire them. Charlie had made it clear he didn't think much of the plan or the mission, but he was willing to accompany them regardless, as long as he was paid in advance.

It occurred to Stefan he wasn't thinking clearly, and perhaps he hadn't been since Shanghai. It was possible he was manic, driven by revenge and ego and pride rather than by logic. But if so, then he'd definitely picked the right team.

Now, here they were, about to confront the creature who had strode through Shanghai, the one Stefan had sunk his fist into, the one that had destroyed the whole city and everyone living there—except those who cowered in the deepest, darkest, safest holes they could find—and had left Stefan alive in the midst of it all. He still didn't understand why the Nemesai had done so. Was it out of some sense of honor or begrudging respect because of the blow he'd landed? Had the beast done it to be cruel? Had it not even considered him as it waded through the carnage?

Stefan didn't know. But the experience had taught him something about their enemy—something not even Atiya had figured out.

The Nemesai were capable of making mistakes.

They'd made one in letting him live.

He was about to prove it to them.

2

"Ninety seconds."

Charlie's voice was calm—almost serene—but Stefan still had to struggle to hear it, even over the headset. The wind noise buffeting the Jeep as they raced down the dirt road made regular conversation impossible.

"I apologize in advance if this doesn't work," Stefan shouted into his microphone.

"Appreciate that," Charlie said, "because it's not going to."

Frankie grinned. "Hell, I'm counting on it not to work. I'm just here for the challenge!"

"Odds are good we'll die," Stefan said.

"Then we die." Frankie shrugged. "It doesn't matter. If I'm dead then I'll be able to sleep again, without those damned dreams. It's the end of the fucking world. Nothing matters anymore."

"The mission still matters," Stefan said. "Remember, if this works, then we go after the other one. If it doesn't work, but we obtain some valuable data, then Charlie takes off and gets that knowledge to somebody who can do something with it."

Both men nodded in confirmation.

"Thirty seconds," Charlie said. "No turning back now."

"We should be able to see it," Frankie yelled.

"We will," Charlie countered.

Stefan didn't doubt him. They had put themselves directly in the thing's path. Charlie had mapped it out, with to the minute updates, based on live data he was receiving from hacking into Russian, Chinese, and

American satellites, and listening to local radio chatter. All of this data went into a computer program he'd designed to worked out times and distances and angles and arcs and even the slope of the roads.

Charlie was good. Maybe not as good as Jude, but good, nevertheless.

They were all good. And the other team, Atiya and fucking Johnson, Jude, Keith, and Christine—they were the best. Fucking aces, that's what they were.

"Charlie," Stefan said, "if this goes sideways, you get the data to Atiya and her team."

"Copy that," Charlie confirmed.

Frankie craned his head over the Jeep's roll cage. "Why can't we see this big fucker?"

Charlie braked, skidding to a stop in the middle of the dirt road, and kicking up clouds of dust and debris. There were trees on either side of them, and hills rolling to every horizon. Dawn was just breaking the nighttime cover.

Stefan and Frankie swung out of the Jeep. Charlie turned it around and sped away, kicking up even more dust.

"Fifteen seconds," he said, still in radio contact.

"Get in position," Stefan said. "We're cutting it close. Make sure you're recording everything."

"Understood."

Frankie took a breath, tightened his fists so hard they popped, rolled his neck left and right, and shouted, "Come dance with me, you motherfucker!"

Stefan remained silent, waiting for the dust cloud to clear.

"Where is it?" Frankie spun in circles, looking. "Where the fuck is it?"

"Hold," Charlie said. The Jeep was now out of sight. "I'm in position, but the satellite...shit."

"What's wrong?" Stefan asked.

"He's stopped. It's like he was waiting for you."

The Nemesai burst through the trees on its snarling mount, sending splinters of timber flying. It paused, drew in a deep breath, and glared down at Stefan.

"Yeah, that's right," Stefan said. "Round two, you son of a bitch."

3

Stefan went in first, as per the plan. Distract the creature, get it focused on him, so Frankie could then wade in and pulverize the thing.

The only problem was the Nemesai seemed to anticipate this.

Stefan slowed as their foe dismounted. It knew. Somehow, it knew what they planned, and it was ready. The Nemesai dropped its long, jagged weapon onto the ground, sending up yet another swirling cloud of dirt. Then it growled.

The mount growled, too, but stepped away.

"Charlie," Stefan said, "are you recording?"

"Affirmative."

The Nemesai stretched out one hand and beckoned.

"Jesus Christ," Charlie muttered. "I told you this was a bad idea…"

Stefan and Frankie charged.

4

Hitting it hurt. Stefan had been in his fair share of fights before. He was no stranger to the shock of pain that ran through one's arms during a punch, how the knuckles and fingers could crack or swell, how shoulders and forearms would ache for days afterward. Those things came with the territory, regardless if you were punching practice bags or another human being. Stefan had hit plenty of both. He knew what it felt like to strike canvas and flesh.

The Nemesai was composed of something different.

The skin of his knuckles split open on the second blow, and after that, every punch he landed splattered his blood across the Nemesai's body. The creature didn't move or fight back, seeming to simply absorb the attack. Stefan aimed for all the known pressure points in its legs, since he couldn't reach beyond the giant's waist, but his carefully placed strikes had no effect. One his seventh punch, Stefan wrenched his shoulder, and his arm went numb. Sweat dripped down his forehead and stung his eyes. He grew winded, and stood panting.

The Nemesai chuckled then, a deep, guttural sound, and struck back, delivering a blow that knocked Stefan off his feet and threw him half a dozen yards. He heard his ribs snap before he felt them. Coughing blood, he slammed into the ground. He tried to raise his head, but his vision was blurry. The only thing he could make out was Frankie wading in, fists balled.

"Let's go, you fuck!"

Stefan winced, stifling a groan as he lifted his head to watch. It hurt to move. Hurt to breathe.

Once again, their opponent declined to fight back.

The creature loomed over Frankie; whose head came even with its waist. Regardless, Frankie hammered the Nemesai wherever he could reach. Three, four, five successive punches into its legs and groin drove the thing back half a step.

Only half a step.

But that was more than anyone else had managed to achieve when fighting it. Artillery hadn't so much as made it flinch, but a punch to the nuts from a mountain of a human being made it stagger.

Grinning, the Nemesai moved with a speed that belied its size, reaching out and seizing Frankie in one massive fist. The big man struggled in its clutch, beating and kicking. His movements grew more frantic as the monster squeezed. Frankie roared, then shrieked. The Nemesai lifted him up, looking him in the eye, and Frankie swung again, battering its nose. Then he reached forward, straining, and scrabbled at the giant's throat with his fingers.

The Nemesai flinched.

Frankie's fingers sank into the flesh. Not much. Just enough to be visible.

"Charlie," Stefan gasped. "Tell me you're getting that."

"Affirmative." Charlie's tone sounded lifeless.

The Nemesai jerked Frankie away from its throat and bit his left arm off at the elbow. Frankie screamed again as the giant crushed him. Blood erupted from his mouth, nose, ears and eyes. His movements ceased, and he went limp. The creature flung his lifeless form aside. Frankie's body slammed against a tree and tumbled to the ground.

The Nemesai turned its attention back to Stefan.

"Shit."

Stefan focused, turning his pain into background ambience. Coughing blood, he staggered to his feet. Each agonizing breath brought a wheezing sound from the left side of his torso. His legs wobbled.

Beckoning, Stefan cursed at the Nemesai in four different languages.

The monster didn't respond. It simply stared, radiating disdain from its contemptuous expression.

Stefan took a faltering step toward it, and then his knees buckled. He toppled over into the grass.

The giant climbed astride its mount and continued on its path unhindered. Both creatures snorted in derision as they rode away.

Stefan closed his eyes and wept.

It had left him alive. Again.

PART FOUR

THE OTHER CITY

1

The stairs, wide enough for five people to walk side by side, spiraled slowly, leisurely, at least fifty meters into darkness.

Leaving Jude and Christine to stand watch at a hut near the top of the stairs, Atiya and Keith led the descent. Johnson and Jane followed behind them.

"Tell me everything you know, Jane," Atiya said.

"*Wo bu zhi dao ren he shi,*" she whispered.

Atiya stopped, halfway down the stairs, and halfway beneath the buried mausoleum. The others halted, as well.

"The silvery rivers, and the stars in the underworld sky," Jane said. "We were told about them as children. That is all I know."

Atiya sighed. "Jude, did you copy that?"

"Affirmative."

"This is what you bring us?"

"She wanted to help," he replied over the radio. "It was a war zone. She needed food and water. You asked for a translator."

"I am sorry," Jane said.

Keith shook his head. "Ease up, Atiya."

Atiya bit back her response and marched more quickly down the stairs. She was on edge and she knew it.

And she did not want to go over.

She heard the footfalls of the others as they followed behind. She stopped again when they reached the bottom, and gaped in wonder.

Johnson gasped. "This place is amazing!"

They stood at the edge of a second underground city. Huge columns and arches supported the weight above them. Roads ran between two-story buildings. Like above, the scattered remnants of recently demolished terracotta warriors were everywhere.

Christine's voice crackled over the radio. "What is it? What did you find?"

Keith grunted. "An underground city beneath an underground city."

Atiya picked up an intact terracotta head. She turned to Jane.

"These statues...why were they so methodically destroyed?"

Jane shrugged. "I do not know. It was said they guarded the emperor."

"But why would the Nemesai eradicate them like this?"

Jane shrugged.

Frowning, Atiya keyed the radio. "Jude, Christine, get down here as soon as you're able. We've got a lot more territory to cover."

"More mercury." Johnson pointed at a nearby flow.

"There's got to be a reason for all of this," Atiya said.

"The emperor thought it would help him live forever," Jane said.

"We know that already," Atiya replied. "There's got to be some other reason."

"Defense?" Keith suggested. He peeked into one of the buildings. They were little more than frames.

Atiya hefted the head. "And all these warriors. Why destroy them?"

"You're re-asking questions," Johnson said.

"Then find me some goddamned answers."

"Here," Keith called, stepping inside the building.

Atiya, Johnson and Jane followed him. The lower halves of two terracotta warriors flanked the doorway. Another pair, more heavily damaged, flanked a wall with a gigantic mural painted on it, rather than canvas or tapestry. The pigments and shades had faded, and were impossible to discern through their breathing apparatus, but the outlines were clear. A hundred warriors in military formation surrounded a monstrous mouth. Swords and spears and bows all pointed inwards, but none looked as sharp as the huge teeth. A ribbon separated the two sides.

"I bet that's silver," Atiya said. "In all the legends and folklore, silver is what they use against evil."

"No," Johnson said. "It's not silver. It's quicksilver. Mercury."

"That's not of the era," Jane whispered.

Everyone turned to her. She was still in the doorway, visibly trembling.

"You've seen it before?" Atiya asked.

Jane shook her head. "No, but I know something about art. This is pre-Chinese."

"What is it" Atiya asked.

"It's old," Johnson replied. "I bet this whole place is older than the city above it. They built the mausoleum overtop it."

"Why?" Atiya asked.

He shrugged.

"There are stories," Jane said, "about gods and devils and dragons and monkey kings, but I've never heard a hint of the Nemesai in any of those stories. Somebody failed."

"Failed?"

Jane pointed at the wall to their right, which everyone had missed because of the painting. Two calligraphic symbols were etched in it, one on top of the other:

Jane wept beneath her mask. "Why didn't they tell us?"

2

The girl sat on the back of the mule. Her grandfather walked beside her. Their cart rattled along behind them.

"Oracle bones?" the girl asked.

"The king took the lower shell of a turtle," her grandfather explained, "scorched it with hot pokers, and divined the future by interpreting the crackles in the shell."

"I bet the turtle wasn't too happy," the girl said.

"I imagine not."

"Do people still do that today?"

Her grandfather shook his head. "We do not have kings any longer."

"I know. But other people. Do they read the oracle bones?"

"If they did, I think the red dreams would've stopped."

They walked in silence for a while before the girl asked, "Are we going to die?"

Her grandfather hesitated to answer.

"Of course," he finally said. "And maybe sooner than we might wish."

The girl nodded, as strongly and wisely and courageously as she could.

"I am not afraid, grandfather."

"I will try not to be, as well."

3

Stefan coughed blood. "The video?"

"It's been sent," Charlie confirmed. "Although I don't know if anyone will learn much from it."

Frowning, Stefan waved in frustration. "Follow it."

Charlie hesitated. "You're in shock, boss."

"Yeah," Stefan replied, "I am. I'm badly injured, and my pride is hurt, and I'm probably going to die. But I don't want to leave the rest of the team alone to face this thing."

"The rest of what team? Frankie's dead, Stefan! Are you talking about Atiya's group? They're not our team."

"Perhaps…but I used to be one of them. You need to tell them. They won't know what we know."

"What we know?" Charlie ran his hands through his close-cropped hair, exasperated. "We don't know shit!"

"You're wrong. If we didn't know anything, you wouldn't have sent the video."

"I sent the video because that's what you fucking paid me to do. I came along on this mission because you hired me. That's what I do. It's my job. But listen to me, Stefan…you're not right in the head. None of this was ever going to work. It was a suicide mission. I figured if you and Frankie wanted to die, okay. Long as I got paid. And I did. But we haven't learned shit. What do you want me to tell Atiya? The Nemesai can be punched. Hip hop hooray, motherfucker! That information won't do them a whole lot of good. Look what it did to you. To Frankie."

"Follow it," Stefan groaned, "or I'll leave you here and follow it myself."

Charlie laughed. "You can't even walk to the Jeep, let alone drive it. Look…we know where it's going. And data shows the other is coming back around, too. When you first called me, you suggested they were on a scouting mission. If that's so, then I guess they've learned whatever they needed to."

"I'd like to teach them something," Stefan said. "Something more than that we're weak. I want to do some damage."

"Fist to fist again?" Charlie asked, shaking his head.

"No. But there's still got to be a way."

"Here." Charlie tilted a bottle of water to Stefan's bloody lips. "Not too much at once, though."

When Stefan was finished, he gasped. "Thanks."

"Punching them didn't work," Charlie said. "Bullets are useless. It's like they absorb the lead."

"Maybe they do."

"And explosives don't even irritate them."

"Bigger explosives, then. Bigger guns. Something other than lead. Silver, maybe?"

"You're not understanding me," Charlie said. "There's nothing we can do. You're in shock now, sure. But I suspect you've been in shock since Shanghai, Stefan. It's time to give this up. I'm going to get you to some help. Maybe save your life. But the Nemesai? You took your shot. Twice now. Shit didn't work out the way you'd hoped. It's over now. There's not a goddamned thing you—or anyone else—can do."

Stefan closed his eyes, and his fists. "We can make sure Atiya doesn't die alone."

Charlie stared at him, and then blinked.

"Yeah," he sighed. "Okay, point. I'd rather not die out here with just your crazy ass for company."

Stefan struggled to sit up. "Then help me to the Jeep."

4

"You can read that?" Atiya pointed at the calligraphy.

Jane nodded. "It too is very old, but I would guess it was etched there some time after the painting."

"So, several generations knew about this place," Johnson mused.

"What does it say?" Atiya asked.

"It says what you've been saying," Jane told her. "What everyone has been calling them. *Nemesai.*"

"Then we've learned something," Atiya said. "Something important."

Johnson frowned. "What's that, exactly?"

"They've been here before," Atiya said. "And they were defeated."

Jane nodded. "By the terracotta army."

"How the hell did a bunch of statues kick their ass?" Keith asked.

Jude's voice came over the radio. "Atiya?"

"Go ahead."

"Remember when I said it was weird we hadn't seen any living things in here—bats or insects?"

"Yeah?"

"Well, we still haven't. But Christine and I *have* found some bodies."

5

Most of the bodies were laid out, side by side, in another hut near the bottom of the stairs. Most had a tablet with what Jane translated as their name engraved upon it. These tablets lay on their collapsed chests. Some of the figures were still covered by tattered, moldering scraps of rags. The bones were well preserved, if mummified in color, but the flesh and organs had long since gone away. Some wore jewels around their necks, gold and jade.

"Who were they?" Atiya asked.

"I would guess they are workers," Jane said. "Not slaves, but laborers of some kind."

"They were left inside?"

"They must've had more work to do," Johnson suggested.

Jane nodded. "So the secrets of their work would be buried with them."

"That wasn't so uncommon," Jude said. "Many ancient cultures did similar things."

"If they had more work to do," Atiya replied, "then what was it?"

Johnson gestured around them. "Building this place?"

Atiya shook her head. "You said yourself, it's older."

"Yes," Jane agreed. "They may have carved the calligraphy, but they were not the builders."

"Someone laid them to rest here.," Atiya stared down at the bodies. "I feel like we're closer to an answer. But we're also running out of time. Everybody check your equipment, make sure everything is still working properly and you're at full charge. Then let's continue.

Teams of two. Jane, you're with me. I'm betting we'll find whatever the hell it is what we're looking for nearby."

"And just what are we looking for, at this point?" Johnson asked.

"Everything."

6

Unlike the level above them, the structures in the sub-subterranean city had at one time been furnished and decorated. Sadly, most of this had since succumbed to the relentless pickings of time. Atiya and Jane found the skeletal remains of chairs and tables and beds. They also came across many remarkably well-preserved tapestries displaying idyllic scenes from above ground — landscapes, public celebrations, and the like.

Atiya paused in front of one showing two children picking berries. A waterfall dominated the background. "What was the point of this?"

"So they would remember the world they came from," Jane guessed.

They found yet another tomb, but unlike the others, this one had been burned. Evidence of fire was widespread, though when and how, Atiya couldn't guess. Inside, the bones had been charred, as had the doorway and roof. Among the remains, they found the blackened bones of children.

"Families?" Jane asked.

Atiya nodded. "They didn't die when they were buried down here. They flourished, for a while. Built themselves an underground civilization."

"But they were sealed in," Jane replied. "How did they eat? Drink? How did they not succumb to the mercury vapor?"

"Who's to say they didn't? Maybe they were a society of mad hatters."

"How many generations lived down here?"

"You're supposed to have answers," Atiya told her. "All I hear are questions."

Jane wheeled around and jabbed Atiya in the chest with her finger. "Do you know how incredibly racist you sound? I told Jude I wanted to help. I didn't know what was involved. Neither did he, I suspect."

"He knew I needed a translator."

"A translator, yes! But not an archaeologist or an expert on ancient civilizations. Just because I am Chinese, that doesn't mean I know anything about this site. Nobody does. It's been sealed up for centuries."

Atiya sighed. "I just…"

"She's right," Jude said over the radio.

"Look…" Atiya paused. "I'm sorry if I came across as…insensitive. That wasn't my intent. I'm tired. We're all tired. And since the dreams started, I guess none of us have been thinking very clearly. I'll try to do better. Okay?"

Jane nodded. "Thank you. So will I."

The two women continued on their way. After a few moments of further exploration, they found an armory, stocked with spears and swords and vicious blades unlike anything Atiya had ever seen. Some were jagged at the end, or had holes cut out of the other side. The frayed remains of what had once been red tassels hung from a few, but not many.

They continued on in silent awe.

There were shops and homes and a room containing jars of herbs and dust and ash.

They found a theatre, with wide stage and a dozen rows of descending seats in a semicircle around it.

And just like the subterranean city above their heads, wherever a terracotta soldier had once stood, there was now only rubble and dust. There was a reason. Atiya couldn't accept it any other way. Had the terracotta warriors actually been meant to protect the world? Were they once alive?

Atiya didn't necessarily discount such phenomena. She'd seen enough things during her career she couldn't explain. But the supernatural wasn't her first go-to. Still, in this case, there was no better explanation. Particularly when giant warriors were roaming the Earth, leaving destruction and slaughter in their wake, and the world's population was sharing a continuous bad dream.

Jude called for a radio check, and their headsets crackled as each team member confirmed their equipment was still working. Jane stepped ahead of Atiya and pointed.

"There, just ahead of us. What is that?"

The building was larger than the others. Atiya went inside first. Jane followed closely. There were a line of workstations, like an assembly line. Clay paint jars, empty now, and ancient brushes lay scattered on a nearby bench. There were several massive kilns and pottery wheels, and wooden wagons covered in what had once been clay.

"What did you find?" Christine asked over the radio.

"It's a factory," Atiya reported. "This is where they made the terracotta warriors."

Jane moved toward a table stacked with weapons and crude, unfinished body parts. Atiya followed her, and picked up one of the heads.

"These aren't the same," she said.

"They're undone," Jane replied.

"Right. Undone. This doesn't have any of the features of the head I found at the stairs. There's a nose, and a mouth, but it's not lifelike."

"Undone," Jane repeated.

"Yes. Undone, and not alive." Atiya sat the head back

on the workbench. "Somebody find me a terracotta warrior they didn't destroy."

Johnson's voice crackled with distortion. "Is that important?"

"Very."

"Then I think I've got something here at the stairs you'll want to see."

"Copy that. We're on our way." Atiya looked at Jane. "Do you believe in God?"

"No. China is a secular nation."

"Yeah, but they recognize five world religions."

"I'm nothing," Jane replied. "No religion."

"What do you believe in, then?"

Jane frowned. "Why?"

"I never believed in God," Atiya said. "Not since my parents were killed in Tripoli."

"I am sorry," Jane said.

"I was a kid. I got over it. I didn't believe in God, and I don't necessarily believe in ghosts, fairies, or the boogeyman."

Jane nodded. "I also don't believe."

"But you believe in the red dreams, obviously?"

"Yes, of course. It would be foolish not to believe in them. All people have the dreams."

"And you've seen the boogeyman," Atiya said. "Up close and personal."

Jane's expression crumpled. "The Nemesai."

Atiya nodded. "Exactly. They're coming back here, and I believe there are more of them. Waiting for the word. And if I believe in that one thing, then I have to be open to all kinds of other beliefs, as well. You follow me?"

Jane frowned in confusion. "I have been following you all along."

"No, I mean do you understand?"

"Yes." Jane nodded.

"So," Atiya continued, "right now, I'm trying to believe the people who lived here long ago did something to help us. Something to protect the world from the Nemesai. But whatever it was, something has since gone terribly wrong. And I have to believe we can fix that, whatever it was. Because otherwise, I don't believe there's any hope left for humanity. You know what it's like out there. People are going insane from the dreams. Entire cities are being destroyed by the Nemesai. I believe we're doomed if we don't figure this out."

"Doomed," Jane repeated, shaking her head. Then, quite suddenly, she said, "I believe in something."

"What's that?"

"I believe in you."

Atiya flinched. "Me?"

Jane nodded again.

"Well, that's…thank you. And look, I'm sorry if I was a bitch to you earlier."

"It's okay." Jane shrugged. "As you said, people are not themselves these days."

No, Atiya thought, *but this is who I was even before the red dreams came…*

"This is all very touching," Johnson said over the radio, "but if you're both done, perhaps you could meet us at the stairs?"

Atiya ground her teeth. Then she winked at Jane.

"But then again," she said, smiling, "Johnson was a bitch long before any of this began."

PART FIVE

THE MOUTH

1

Atiya stood, marveling. "Tell me again how you found it?"

"We were rigging explosives at the top of the stairs," Christine explained, "like you said to."

Johnson waved his hand dismissively. "Although I don't know what good explosives would do against those things."

"Well, they sure won't hurt to try," Keith argued.

Atiya held up a hand, silencing them both. Then she nodded at Christine. "Go on."

"Well, we were just about to set more at at the bottom when we found the door. It was under the stairs, and hidden in the shadows."

"And it's the only door in this whole goddamned place," Keith said.

"We forced it open. It took some effort, as you can see from the ruts in the floor." Christine pointed. "One of the hinges snapped. But we found these."

Atiya walked around the two wholly intact terracotta warriors, examining them, amazed at how pristine they were. They appeared to be better preserved than the army uncovered at Xi'an. Sure, time had weathered them. Only a trace of their paint still remained, but their eyes appeared so lifelike, even now.

And their weapons were still sharp.

"What do we do with them?" Johnson asked.

Atiya gently touched one of the warriors. He felt so fragile beneath her palm. "I don't know. But they're important."

"Historically, or archeologically?" Johnson snorted. "Because I don't see how either matters a whole fucking lot right now."

"They're meant to protect us," Atiya said. "Somehow."

"Bullshit!" Johnson sneered. "You're making this up as you go along, Atiya. You've got no idea. No plan. These things aren't protecting shit."

"Easy, Johnson…" Jude held up his hands in a placating gesture. "You're exhausted. We all are. It's easy to be frustrated. But Atiya has never led us wrong before. We need to—"

Johnson swung, broadly and without malice, at the lower half of the closest terracotta warrior. The statue shattered. Its head tilted to the side as it went down, and in that moment, it seemed almost alive—and confused. Its weapon fell, clattering amidst the shards on the floor.

"There." Johnson put his hands on his hips and nodded in smug satisfaction. "A lot of good they'll do us."

Atiya moved fast, shoving him backwards, away from the other statue, and slammed him into the wall. She heard Johnson's teeth clack together, and saw blood squirt from his lips beneath the gas mask. Before he could react, she drew her pistol and shoved it under his chin, in the soft part of his throat. She was keenly aware the rest of the team were watching, unmoving. Jane whimpered. The others were silent.

Then she realized Johnson was laughing.

"You have no authority over me," he said.

Atiya glared at him, though it was hard to convey her attempt through the gas mask.

"It's okay," Jude assured Jane.

Atiya's finger tightened on the trigger. She could get rid of a lot of problems, right here and now. Chances were, they'd never need his particular talents again. And even if they did, she could find another to fill his role. The world was full of fast-talking charmers and face men.

"Give me one reason," Atiya said, "not to shoot you right here and now."

He still laughed, though not very heartily. "I'm vital. You need me."

"No," Atiya said, pulling the trigger. "We don't."

He dropped.

Jane screamed.

The spent brass cartridge flew from her gun and landed amidst the terracotta shards.

The spray of Johnson's blood on the wall seemed to almost glow when viewed through their masks.

Atiya holstered the still smoking pistol. Jane held both hands over her mouth. Keith and Jude stared down at Johnson's corpse. Christine's eyes were on Atiya.

"Do we have a problem?" Atiya asked.

"Nope," Christine said. "No problem. He was always an asshole."

"I…" Jude paused, sighing.

Atiya turned to him. "Yeah?"

He shook his head. "Nothing. No problem."

"Good." Atiya turned back to the remaining terracotta warrior. "Let's figure this thing out. Jane, find…"

She turned, but Jane was backing toward the door. Atiya grabbed her by the arm and yanked her toward the statue.

"Hey," Jude protested. "Atiya, this isn't—"

"Find some writing or something on the warrior," Atiya said.

"You want her to find the instruction manual?" Jude's tone was incredulous.

"That's why we're here, isn't it?"

"Atiya…" Jude paused again. "Maybe we should check the seals on your mask. Because the way you're acting right now…"

"Just do it," she ordered. "Spread out. I want this entire level searched. We're out of time."

2

Christine knew Atiya had a history with Johnson that probably matched her own—a series of unwanted, predatory sexual advances. She had never told Keith, because that would have just caused more trouble, and besides, she'd dealt with it well enough. Christine was strong enough to not simply reject Johnson, but, at times, put him in his place physically (and painfully). Although that had never seemed to deter him. Probably, he'd gotten off on it. Fucker.

So she felt no regret, and no pity at his death; but also, she felt no joy. The atmosphere didn't allow for that. They'd all come here knowing they would probably die.

Johnson, true to form, had talked his way out of it and escaped before the fighting got ugly.

3

"Atiya."

"Yes, Jude?"

There was a burst of static. "Keith and I found something interesting."

"There's a whole lot interesting down here," Atiya said, "but we're running low on useful. What is it?"

Jude hesitated, then said, "The mouth."

4

The girl and her grandfather were now near the Lintong Mortuary Complex.

"So, Ying Zhèng saved us when he was king," the girl said, "and then defeated all his enemies to unite China. How?"

"After overcoming our truest enemies," her grandfather replied, "and sealing them again in the earth's core, and creating an army to face them should they rise again, all other challenges were insignificant."

"They tried to assassinate him," the girl said.

"You watch too many movies."

"No, a man with a poison dagger," she insisted. "I read it in school. I learned it. I didn't see it in a movie."

"Good," her grandfather said, pride welling up in his throat and stopping all other words. "Good."

"Are we going to defeat them? You and I? Is that where we're going?"

Her grandfather shook his head. "No. We're going to watch them rise out of the ground, because it is our duty to be witnesses."

"But haven't we witnessed enough already?"

Nodding, he patted her head. "Our people forgot. One day, when you are my age, it might fall on you to remind future generations. So, we will watch. From a safe distance. And if the Ancestors are kind and forgiving, perhaps they will ignore us entirely."

"They were beaten once," the girl said. "We have better armies now, don't we?"

"We have forgotten what is necessary."

"You mean they have forgotten," the girl said. "But you remember, don't you?"

He smiled sadly. "No."

"What about his army? The ones meant to defend us?"

"As emperor, Qin Shi Huangdi spent a lot of time pursuing immortality. He would've kept his chancellor, our Ancestor, at his side, and he would've kept his entire army."

"Then he should still be emperor."

"He failed," her grandfather said. "His soldiers turned first to stone, then dust, then back to stone, and I think all that remains of them now are the terracotta warriors in a museum in Xi'an."

"Oh," said the girl.

And that was, for a long while, the end of their conversation.

5

It took Atiya ten minutes to reach Jude and Keith. They were perched in the perimeter of a large gate, their posture tense, their weapons held at the ready. The gate itself was made of iron, partially rusted but not nearly so bad as it should be, assuming it was erected thousands of years ago. The mouth beyond it was huge, larger than the Lincoln Tunnel, big enough for tanks and planes to pour through.

Or a Nemesai.

The gate stood open.

And in the opening, lay a giant corpse.

Atiya pointed. "Is that…?"

"Nemesai," Jude confirmed.

"Dead?"

"Looks dead," Keith said, "but we haven't exactly gone in to make sure. You never watch a horror film?"

"And all around it," Jude said, "broken pieces of those terracotta warriors. The fragments aren't dusty. They're recent."

"What do you think?" Atiya asked. "What can we surmise?"

"I think," Jude said, hesitating and returning his gaze to the Nemesai corpse. "There was a fight."

"What killed it?"

"Can't be certain."

"We need to get closer."

"Horror films, remember," Keith said.

"Cover us," Atiya told him. "Jude, you're with me."

She and Jude crept slowly toward the corpse. There was no cover, no place to hide, no place to run, and Atiya was all-too-aware just how exposed they were. If anything else was alive inside the tunnel, Nemesai or otherwise, they would be seen, and they would have no defense.

When they reached the giant, she knelt, examining the body. Slash marks were visible up and down its length.

"Those wounds look burned." Jude prodded a gash with the tip of his sidearm.

"Doesn't look like fire, though," Atiya said.

"Acid of some sort, would be my guess."

"So," Atiya said, standing. "Something useful at last."

"How so?"

"Now we're sure they're not impervious." She stared into the long, dark tunnel beyond the gate. It sloped down more deeply, into the very core of the earth.

"Get topside," Atiya said. "Let people know. Tell whoever will listen. Start with the Chinese authorities. Take Jane with you. Jane, do you copy that?"

"I understand." Her voice was muffled over the radio.

Jude shook his head. "But we don't yet know what kind..."

"Then tell them that, too," Atiya interrupted. "Tell them where we are. Tell them everything we know so far!"

"What will you do?" Jude asked.

She stared up at the open gate. Iron prongs hung like gleaming teeth. She saw no sign of a counterweight.

"I'm going to close this gate."

5

After studying it some more, Atiya surmised the gate's mechanisms had to be in one of the nearby buildings. Unlike the other underground dwellings they'd encountered so far, the structures near the tunnel all stood three stories high, with plenty of windows looking over the mouth.

She stood there listening, peering into the dark depths of the tunnel. Then she held her breath. Although the sounds were muffled through her protective gear, Atiya was certain there were noises in that darkness. Echoes of far-off grunts and what sounded like a blacksmith pounding on metal. The ground periodically vibrated beneath her feet.

Fortifying the gate seemed at best a stopgap measure. They'd buy time, but merely delay the inevitable, because if all of the Nemesai were as powerful as their scouts, impervious to gunfire and bombs and missiles and everything else the Chinese army had thrown at them, three inch thick iron bars weren't going to stop them.

It was something, though. They had so little of anything.

"Keith," she said into the radio, "get down here and help me find the controls to this gate."

"You sure you don't want me to cover you from up here?"

She looked up in his direction, though he was too far away to see. "I've never known you to be scared, Keith."

"The hell you haven't," he responded. "Only a bullshit artist like Johnson would claim they're never scared. So save your reverse psychology, Atiya. It's nothing like that. I just want to get a few shots off before it's too late. Easier to do that from this vantage point."

"Shots didn't save Shanghai," Atiya said. "Get down here."

"Copy. On my way."

Atiya stood waiting, trying her best to ignore the sounds and vibrations beneath her feet.

Christine cleared her throat over the microphone.

"Everything okay?" Atiya asked.

"Yeah," Christine replied. "I'm just wondering…are we sure our breathing apparatus are working properly? We all seem…I don't know."

Nobody responded.

"We were already loopy, even before we came down here," Atiya replied. "I don't think the mercury vapors would affect us that quickly. If we're not behaving like ourselves, I'd say it's more likely the stress of what's going on in the world finally taking its toll on us."

"I'm going offline," Jude reported. "Taking my mask off while topside. I'll radio when I'm back on comms."

"Copy that," Atiya said.

Keith appeared, walking slowly and choosing his footing carefully. He kept his gun trained on the corpse as he approached.

"You sure that thing is dead?"

Atiya nodded. "It's dead."

"Then we can kill them."

"First we need to figure out what killed it," Atiya said. "Jude thinks it was acid. I tend to agree. Do you have any ideas?"

Keith didn't touch the creature, but he studied it for a long time. His posture was tense. Finally, he lowered his weapon and relaxed.

"Thoughts?"

"You might be right about the acid," he agreed. "Definitely not bullets, I guess. But I still want to shoot one of them."

"You'll get your chance," Atiya told him.

7

Topside, Jude sent the information to other freelance mercenaries, private security firms, researchers and universities, media outlets, fringe journalists, and various militaries, governments, and intelligence agencies. He sent the message in nine languages—each that he knew—and of course asked people to pass it on and make it go viral. He knew some of the recipients would disregard it as a hoax or the ravings of some internet crackpot, but other people—important people who sat on the review boards at various labs or called the shots in various military chains-of-command—knew who he was.

He leaned back, sighed, and stared at the sky. His face was chafed from wearing the mask for so long, and he dreaded donning it again. The breeze felt good against his skin. He closed his eyes, and focused on letting the stress drain from him. He visualized it as water running out of his body and seeping into the soil. Then he thought of Johnson's blood leaking out in the catacombs below, and he frowned.

He heard a distant rumbling that sounded like thunder—but wasn't.

The scouts were returning.

I could stay here, he thought. *I could just sit here and meditate and let it squash me.*

If it had just been him, he might have done just that. But there was Atiya and Keith and Christine to think about. And Jane. He was responsible for getting her into this mess. He had to at least warn them.

Sighing again, he stood up and repacked his equipment. He was about to stow his portable radio, when a voice came over it.

"Jude? If you're reading me, your people have an ETA of sixty minutes. Maybe less."

He frowned. "Who's this?"

"Who do you think? I know it's been a while since we worked together, but come on."

"Charlie?"

"Affirmative."

"Charlie…" Jude paused in confusion. "Last I heard, you were in Tulsa. What are you doing here?"

"We're following one of the bastards now. It killed Frankie."

"Who's we?"

"Me and Stefan."

"Stefan? So he's alive after all?"

"Affirmative. Although I don't know for how long."

"What do you—"

"Jude," Charlie interrupted, "we can play catch up later. Right now, you're about to have company."

"Only sixty minutes?" Jude asked. "I thought we'd have longer."

"You thought wrong."

"Any good news for me?" Jude asked. "I've been underground."

"Nothing good, no. You?"

"You see the message I just sent out?"

"Stefan read it to me. I'm a little busy multitasking at the moment."

"Well," Jude said, "that's what we know. Something killed one of them."

"Then you've had better results than we have. How many more are there? Any idea?"

"I don't know," Jude admitted. "Atiya thinks there's an army waiting down there."

"And you?"

"I'm beginning to think she's right."

Sighing a third time, he donned his protective equipment and glanced at the sky once more, wondering if he'd ever see it again.

Then he headed underground.

8

They found the wooden mechanics responsible for lifting and lowering the gate. It had been smashed. The thick rope was shredded, leaving only frayed strands hanging from the ceiling.

"It ain't moving," Keith grunted.

They were on the second story of the building adjacent to the gate, and could see deeper into its maw from here. It looked more like a mouth now, and Atiya couldn't help but glance to the ceiling, looking for a pair of blinking eyes to go with it.

She took a deep breath, tore herself away from the window and focused on the splintered equipment.

"It's jammed," Keith said. "Going nowhere."

"That's not a worst-case scenario."

"Why not?"

"Because they'll have to crawl to get through."

"And while they're on the floor and vulnerable," Keith said, "we can kick sand in their eyes. Unless you've got some acid on standby you didn't tell us about."

"There's got to be other defenses." Atiya motioned with a sweep of her hand. "This whole place was built to keep them out."

"They obviously got out. Assuming you're right, it looks like the last defenses have fallen."

Jude's voice came over the radio. "Company's coming, folks. Get into your Sunday best. We've got an hour. Maybe less."

"That's not a lot of time," Christine said. She sounded so defeated. So unlike herself.

"You told me we had way more than that," Atiya said into her radio.

"Yeah, well, I was wrong. We don't."

9

Jane ignored the chatter of the others. If she paid attention to what they were saying and translating it in her head, then she couldn't focus on what she'd found—a massive, well-preserved tapestry that, through the use of painted caricatures, told the story of the Nemesai. So while Jude, Atiya, Christine and Keith argued with each other—seemingly unaware of the rising panic mirrored in each of their voices—Jane studied. She learned the Nemesai came up from the bowels of the earth, razed the farms and villages, and took no prisoners. They had risen many thousands of years ago, and were fought by an army that predated the Bronze Age Shang dynasty. They rose again thousands of years later, to be once again beaten and driven back. When they rose a third time, the first Emperor of China built this city to defend it.

Twenty thousand warriors had lived here, underground.

Jane went to one of the quicksilver rivers, knelt, and removed her gloves. She remembered Atiya's warning about how mercury could be absorbed through the skin, but at that moment, she didn't care. Staring with wonder, she cupped her hand, and lifted some of the liquid metal. She was surprised by how heavy the silvery-white substance was, and how cool it felt. She'd assumed it would be hot, bubbling up from the bowels of the earth. Most of it dissolved into her skin. Frowning, she tried again, with the same result.

She glanced up at the mural, and her frown slowly turned into an astonished smile.

She didn't have a cup, but after a quick search of her surrounding, Jane found a piece of a broken terracotta warrior that might work.

She dipped it into the mercury.

It, too, absorbed the metal, though not as quickly.

"*Bu*," she said, angry now.

After a few minutes of searching, she found a deeper, more bowl-like fragment, one that might hold the mercury long enough to serve her experiment.

She dipped it into the river and then hurried back to the room under the stairs. Johnson's corpse lay cooling on the floor. She stepped over him and dumped what little mercury the makeshift bowl hadn't absorbed on the statue's head.

It was the only whole terracotta warrior left.

For a moment, nothing happened.

Jane cursed.

And then the warrior blinked.

PART SIX

PLAN C

1

"What do we have for a line of defense?" Atiya asked, as she and Keith double-timed it back to the staircase.

"The explosives are set," Christine replied.

"At least that's something," Atiya said. "Maybe we can close this place off. Got any more of that good stuff, Christine?"

"Not much."

"Enough to blow shut the mouth?" Atiya asked.

"That's what…about the size of a DC-10?"

"Affirmative," Keith answered.

"No," Christine said. "Not that much."

"Then we'll make do with what we've got," Atiya decided. "Make sure the staircase is coming down."

"And a big section of the city above us," Christine said.

"Good."

"Won't be enough," Keith said between steps. "That'll only slow them down."

"Those iron bars held them, once," Atiya argued. "You don't think a few tons of rock will stand in their way?"

"No."

"Such an optimist," Atiya panted.

"What we need," Keith said, "is more help and more time."

"Sorry," Jude's response sounded far off. "We're out of both."

Then, Jane's voice broke in over the chatter, small and tentative. "I…I think I have some help."

2

"It's not much," Jane said, as they circled the terracotta warrior. "But it moved."

"Moved?" Atiya scowled. "Like, it walked?"

"It blinked."

"You're right," Atiya said. "That's not much."

"It *moved*," Jane said. "I think that's a lot more than not much."

"You said it blinked. Blinking isn't going to do us much good against the Nemesai!"

"After all your talk of belief," Jane scolded. "I thought you were different. I should have known better."

"Okay." Atiya leaning close to examine the face. "You stay here and see if you can make him move again. If he does anything useful besides blinking, let us know. In the meantime, I've got a plan."

"Is it a good plan?" Christine asked.

"No," Atiya admitted. "but it's a plan. Everybody listen up."

3

Jude was halfway down the long descent, retracing his steps through the subterranean maze, and hurrying to find the rest of the team when the world shook above him.

"Shit," he muttered into the radio. "Here we go, gang."

4

Charlie and Stefan skidded to a stop along the outer rim of the massive burial mound. A cloud of dust and debris billowed around the structure, emanating from a freshly made hole big enough to drive several buses through. Charlie killed the engine and keyed the radio.

"Jude," he said, "if you can still read me, time's up. Our friend is in. I say again, he's in. And the second one should be here any—"

Stefan didn't wait for Charlie to finish. Groaning, he slumped out of the Jeep and shuffled toward the hole the Nemesai had been kind enough to smash through the earth. He clutched an MP5 in his hands, and a long knife dangled from his belt. He knew neither of them would do any good against their opponent, but having them made him feel better, regardless.

He heard Jude's muffled, distorted response come over the radio. Heard Charlie ask him to repeat it.

Then the forest exploded, and something crashed through the trees.

Stefan glanced back, but didn't even have time to yell a warning. The second Nemesai swung down at the Jeep with its free hand, not even bothering with the weapon it carried, crushing both the vehicle and Charlie with it. Sparks flew. Motor oil, gasoline, and blood sprayed. Metal shrieked and so did Charlie.

The Nemesai roared. It sounded like a lion, or an elephant, or a whale—some combination of all these and more. The sound roiled like thunder. It reverberated in Stefan's bones, shaking his teeth, as bits of rock and dirt rattled at his feet. He stared, motionless, getting a good look at what was inside the giant's mouth—teeth like spikes, jagged and discolored and pointing in random directions.

Roaring a second time, the Nemesai lifted the crumpled Jeep and tossed it aside. Charlie's mangled body landed at its feet like a diminutive ragdoll. Then, as if remembering it was armed, the creature pointed its long, sharp blade at Stefan.

"Fuck you, too." Talking hurt. So did moving, for that matter, but he limped toward the opening, walking backwards. His gaze never left his enemy.

It occurred to him then the lower half of the giant's mount was missing. Where had it gone?

Catlike, the Nemesai leapt forward. The ground shook when it landed. Stefan heard dirt sliding down behind him.

Shrugging, he stopped, spread his feet apart and opened fire. His aim was off, but some of the burst hit his target. He knew the attack would have no effect, but it distracted the giant long enough for him to slip through the opening in the earth. As the Nemesai lumbered forward, he slid under the monster's reach and down toward the edge of the underground city.

He scrabbled for purchase amidst the dirt and rocks, narrowly managing to avoid falling into a river of quicksilver. He could barely see, but the mercury gave off a weak iridescence.

Then, even that meager illumination disappeared, as the Nemesai surged through the hole in pursuit. Once again, Stefan was bewildered by its speed. He opened fire as it loomed over him, emptying the rest of his ammo into the giant's groin, assuming it had one. The creature seemed entirely unaffected. It leaned close, huge red eyes aglow.

Stefan pulled his knife and thrust it upwards. The

blade glanced off its hide.

"Well…" He spat blood and coughed. "I tried, at least."

The Nemesai shoved its blade down, piercing Stefan's abdomen, and the earth beneath him, and buried the weapon to its hilt. Stefan bit back a scream, tried not to squirm, tried to keep his eyes focused on the thing about to kill him.

Instead, the Nemesai left him there, pinned to the ground, helpless and useless, and dying in agony like a butterfly on a pin.

5

"Jude," Atiya said, "give me a sitrep."

"Standby," he whispered over the radio.

She had to strain to hear him. Then she heard something else, above them. The Nemesai, lumbering about like a monster in a kaiju film.

Jude remained upstairs, in the first underground city, hidden in one of the many empty buildings. The plan was to radio when both Nemesai had gone down the stairs. Then Christine, who was also hidden, would blow them. Atiya and Keith's job was to slow the first one down until the second came through. Both Atiya and Keith occupied a perch facing either side of the stairs, mustered at angles so they wouldn't risk hitting each other with friendly fire.

The ponderous, thudding footfalls grew louder. Dust and dirt rained down upon them.

"Okay," Jude whispered. "Target is descending."

The warning was unnecessary. The entire area shook with its approach.

"Jane," Atiya said, "you need to quit messing around with that statue and get clear. You're out of time."

There was no response.

"Jane? Do you copy?"

Silence.

"Shit. Christine? Jude? Do you have eyes on her?"

"Negative," Christine replied.

"She's not up here," Jude reported.

"Look," Keith muttered. "We've got company. We'll have to worry about her later."

Atiya focused her aim near the center of the staircase. Keith did the same. They knew their bullets would do no good against the enemy, but they hoped the barrage would provide a distraction. Their goal was to keep the Nemesai on the stairs for as long as possible. When the second one arrived and joined it, Christine would blow the explosives. The plan's major flaw, as Keith had pointed out, was they had no idea how long they'd have to wait for the second Nemesai to arrive. Should everything go sideways—which Atiya assumed it would—they would blow the staircase anyway, burying the mouth and making it that much harder for the Nemesai army in the depths of the earth to claw their way to the surface.

But none of that had involved burying Jane with them.

A great cloud of dust and dirt roiled at the bottom of the staircase. Then, slowly, the Nemesai emerged.

Keith opened fire. The Nemesai stopped, scowling in annoyance at the rounds bouncing off it.

Atiya delivered a controlled burst.

The Nemesai put its hands on its hips and laughed. The sound hurt Atiya's ears.

6

Jane brought more and more mercury to the terracotta warrior. It shifted a finger. It blinked again. Then it parted its lips, as if to speak, or to breathe.

Ignoring the sounds of gunfire, she brought more.

So much quicksilver seeped into her skin, much more than she would've believed possible in so quick a time.

Finally, the warrior spoke.

"*Sha di?*" Its voice was gravely, dust-dry, difficult to discern.

Jane nodded.

But the warrior said nothing more.

"You must help us," Jane whispered, hugging the statue, as if her nearness alone might give it life.

The warrior said, "*Bang zhu.*"

Jane wiped a tear from her eye.

The tear glimmered on her fingertip.

7

"Second target is on site," Jude reported. "He's coming down. No mount, just like the other, which means they're probably still topside."

"Copy." Atiya felt both relieved and overwhelmed.

In an effort to delay the first Nemesai, she and Keith had shot at the walls and the stairs themselves, eroding the structural integrity enough to bring rocks and debris raining down on their opponent. As it emerged from the rubble, it looked at them both and snarled.

"I'm empty," Keith yelled.

"I'm almost, too," Atiya replied. "But we…wait. I see it! The second one is on its way down the stairs. Do it, Christine!"

"Are you two clear? Does anyone have eyes on Jane?"

"Never mind us," Atiya shouted. "Just fucking blow it!"

The top of the stairs exploded, and a new deluge of debris rained down.

Atiya resisted the urge to shield her eyes.

Both of the Nemesai fell, buried beneath stone and dirt.

8

Jane screamed as stones crashed through the ceiling. She jumped back, through the door, as one particularly large boulder shattered the terracotta warrior she'd been bringing to life.

Distraught, she blamed herself for its destruction. She shouldn't have been there. She'd heard Atiya over the radio, telling her to move, that time was up, but she'd ignored the warnings because she thought the Westerner's plans were futile.

Jane was convinced their only hope was in reviving the terracotta warrior.

She felt connected to it, both its descendant and mother. They were of the same nation, of the same culture. They were survivors, she and the warrior, and if she could just nurse him back from whatever had entombed him in terracotta, the warrior could then fight for her, beat back the Nemesai, stand not just for China but for the world.

Nothing less would save them.

And now…it was gone. Destroyed, just like all the others.

It felt like her heart shattered along with the terracotta fragments.

A moment later, her bones shattered as well, as everything above smashed down upon her. An avalanche of rocks, dirt, masonry and other debris poured into the chamber, choking the air and blinding her vision.

The Nemesai came with it all.

One landed near her. She felt it, rather than saw it. Its labored breathing sounded like a train rumbling up a hill. Jane couldn't breathe. She ripped off her mask, gulped air, and held it, afraid to make a sound. She tasted blood in her mouth.

Then, the floor plummeted out from under her, and she pinwheeled into the darkness below.

She fell for what seemed like a long time before striking a hard surface. The pain was so intense she couldn't even scream. Then she realized, as she began to sink and flail, she'd fallen into a mercury river.

PART SEVEN

JANE

1

The pain vanished.

Jane's fear went with it, replaced by an overwhelming sense of calm.

The liquid felt strange around her, cold and thick. It seeped into her mouth, her eyes, her pores. It wasn't like drowning, it was like losing herself to a nightmare. She had no sense of up or down. Absolute silence engulfed her.

And madness.

In her mind's eye, she saw an army of Nemesai marching toward an iron gate. She saw terracotta warriors standing their ground, forcing the beasts back. She saw the gates closed. She saw the drums ripped apart.

She heard nothing, and it was deafening.

Cold oozed into her. Numbness. She reached out for something, but there was nothing to grab, nothing to hold, nothing to find.

She kicked, without effect.

She floated.

And as she floated, she remembered monkey kings and dragons, she recalled stories of the Yellow River babbling as a girl walked away. She saw the bridge built, and the Shaolin training in the shadow of some non-existent temple. She saw tiered fields of rice, and fireworks exploding, and a craftsman finishing a vase. She saw opium dens and Japanese soldiers and felt the fatal cold of Himalayan peaks. She saw Tang poets bending words, and a bearded man playing an erhu. Beijing opera and Lion dances, bright red and gold and white glove puppets, and dragon boats and swordsmen and...

...and she saw the Chinese soldiers hacking Nemesai to bits with their quicksilver swords and spears, the king shouting out orders, even the chancellor burying blades to the hilt in the unforgiving flesh of the Nemesai, the army driving the creatures back, deeper into their cave, a cave which they later sealed, knowing the Nemesai would return yet again...

Forgetting where she was, Jane gasped for breath, and swallowed another mouthful of mercury instead.

And then she saw red. Red dreams. The red dreams that had come before the Nemesai. A portent. An omen. A warning. Who had sent them? How? Why? Jane knew, but she didn't really know how she knew, and further, she didn't really care because she found herself sinking deeper and deeper into the mercurial red.

Deeper, and deeper still.

2

Christine set off the second set of explosives.

The bottom of the stairs, and the pile of rubble atop them, erupted in a fireball.

Even with her eyes closed, Atiya saw the flash.

"Report," she coughed. "Did we bury them?"

Silence followed. Groaning, Atiya abandoned her perch, heading back to the ground.

Keith's voice came over the radio. "I can't see any movement."

"I think we got them," Christine said.

"It's good to hear you," Keith told her.

"It's good to hear you, too." The radio did nothing to conceal Christine's tears.

Atiya clambered across heaps of rubble. "Jude?"

He didn't answer.

Which was, hopefully, because he'd already gone back to the surface to let the Chinese government know where to drop the nukes and maybe seal this hole.

"Jane?" she asked.

Again, no answer.

"Christine, do you have eyes on either of them?"

"Negative."

"Does it matter?' Keith asked. "None of us are getting out of here now."

"Atiya?"

She gasped. It was Stefan's voice. He sounded weak and distant.

"Stefan? Where are you? How did you—"

"Never mind that… Sounds like you…did some damage. I hope it was enough…to hurt them."

"Where are you?" Atiya glanced around, bewildered. "You're close."

"I'm under," he said. "Just wanted...to say...I'm done...it...it didn't kill me...but...left me...to die..."

"We all die today." Atiya's voice cracked. "And we all die well, soldier."

"Not...soldier," Stefan gasped, voice dripping with pain. "Lover...lover."

Atiya closed her eyes. "Lover."

Stefan said no more.

The Nemesai, both simultaneously, erupted from their burial mound of stone and stairs. Fires burned around them, despite the fact there was little combustible material around them to burn. They glowed red, no different than the red of the dreams. Their eyes reflected the darkest depths. Their grins were inhuman. Even dismounted, even without their horse-beasts, they loomed over everything else.

Gouts of quicksilver bubbled up through the debris, trickling across the rubble. Both creatures gave the splashes a wide berth. Then, a veritable mercury fountain began to spout behind them. Moving away from it, the Nemesai turned their attention back to their opponents.

Atiya tossed her empty gun aside. Her shoulders slumped.

Keith moved beside her. "Screw that. I'll go out clobbering one of them with mine if I have to."

Smiling, Atiya rested her hand on his shoulder and squeezed.

"I'm on my way down," Christine said. "Don't die without me."

As the Nemesai glowered at her, Atiya took a deep breath and squared her shoulders.

"We'll do our best," she muttered, "but you'd better hurry."

And then something reached out of the fountain of quicksilver.

3

Atiya gaped. When she saw Jane pulling herself out of the liquid metal, she couldn't do much of anything else.

So, too, did Keith. He was barely aware of Christine as she rejoined them and took his hand. Then, she stared as well.

The Nemesai, perhaps confused by their reaction, turned around to look as Jane stood up behind them.

She glowed. Her fingernails were silvery, and her eyes, and her hair. She grinned. It was no smile, but a wicked, nasty, mischievous—and, ultimately, *mad*—expression she wore.

She said something in Chinese, fast and soft, maybe a prayer or a curse, or maybe a warning to the Nemesai. Whichever, it ended quickly, and then she threw herself at the nearest of the Nemesai.

She grabbed its back, screaming and cackling, her incoherent words a mix of Mandarin and Cantonese and Shanghainese and English and German. She pummeled the back of the creature, her tiny little arms swinging wildly and relentlessly. The giant reached for her, but the effort was futile. Jane was too fast. She buried her hand in the back of the creature's neck.

The Nemesai jittered, as if shocked. It tried to buck her, as a rodeo bull might, leaping and twisting and reaching behind its back. And it screamed. This was no howl or roar, but an agonized, high-pitched screech. The noise hurt Atiya's ears, but she loved it.

She didn't know exactly what was happening, or why or how, but it didn't take a lot of effort to put pieces together.

The Nemesai had a poison. A kryptonite. Mercury.

The answer had been right here all around them the entire time.

"Jude," she said into her radio. "Jude, goddamn it, answer me."

The Nemesai dropped to its knees. Its scream turned into a keening, pitiful wail.

Laughing, Jane ripped something wet and sloppy out of its head. Then she turned to face the other.

The remaining Nemesai greeted her with its weapon. As she ran toward it, the giant struck, driving the blade through her chest, then slicing upward to cut a chunk of her torso away. Without pause, it struck downward, hacking off her arm.

"No," Christine screamed.

Jane remained standing, slowly swaying back and forth. She bled quicksilver.

Keith raised his rifle and squeezed the trigger, but there was only an empty click. He didn't seem to notice. He kept aiming and dry firing.

Another twist of its weapon, and the Nemesai decapitated Jane. Mercury spouted from the stump where her head had been.

Atiya shouted for Jude, but there was still no response.

The Nemesai bounded away toward the mouth.

"Jude," Atiya screamed into her radio. "Stefan! Charlie! Someone!"

"They're not answering," Keith said. "And pretty soon that thing is going to lead a legion of its brothers back through that hole. We have to stop it. We know how now."

"Jane is dead," Christine pointed out. "Whatever the mercury did for her, it didn't made her invulnerable."

Atiya shook her head. "Christine, how big a hole can you still make?"

"I can make a hole," Christine said.

"We need to divert one of these mercury flows," Atiya said.

"Divert it where?" Christine asked.

"Into the mouth."

4

The Nemesai had bent and cracked many of the iron teeth in the mouth as it fled. The spurting mercury fountains, and the new streams they were forming, did not pass very close to the opening. They were more of a perimeter around it, a defensive line but not the first. The ground was too level.

"We should have done this to start with," Keith said.

"But that wouldn't have stopped the two scouts," Atiya reminded him. "And besides, we didn't know about the quicksilver then."

He shrugged. "We should have."

"Look," Atiya snapped. "We've already established none of us are thinking clearly. Let's just focus on this. Christine, how is it looking?"

"Blow a hole big enough to divert one of those flows?" Christine shook her head. "Can't be done. Not with what I've got left."

"We can dip our ammo into the mercury," Keith suggested. "That'll be enough to do some damage."

"We don't have any ammunition left, remember?" Atiya sighed.

"I do," Christine said. "Not much, but more than I have left in explosives."

"Can we dig?" Keith asked. "Make a little trench of something?"

"The dirt is too hard," Atiya replied. "Especially without shovels. If we can't get the quicksilver flowing down into that throat, can we at least—?"

Drums sounded below, sounding like thunderclaps deep beneath the earth.

The sound was followed by marching feet. Distant.

And very slow. But they ascended, and there must've been thousands of them, thousands of Nemesai rising from the very heart of the earth, from an unknown and unknowable history.

"We should go for a swim," Keith said. "Give us a fighting chance. None of us are getting out of here, anyhow."

"You're right," Atiya said. "But we need...we need to somehow let someone else know how to fight them. Someone outside of the three of us. Because we alone will not stop their army. You saw what happened to Jane."

"We can give them one hell of a fight," Keith said.

"I..." Atiya paused.

"He's right," Christine said softly. "No exit strategies remain, Atiya. This is where and how we die."

"But all those people on the surface —"

"Aren't our problem now." Christine took Atiya's hand and squeezed it. "Someone else will have to figure it out. We tried. We failed. But maybe we can win in choosing how we go out."

Atiya nodded. "We hold them off, as best we can. We show them Hell."

Keith walked over to a spouting geyser of mercury, and stared into the flow. Then he turned back to them and slowly removed his breathing apparatus. He smiled.

"I'd say ladies first, but I was never that guy. Christine...I love you."

"I love you, too."

He nodded. "Atiya?"

She returned the gesture.

"Okay, then. See you both in a second."

Still grinning, he jumped into the crack in the earth and sank into the pool.

5

As Keith inhaled his last breath of mercury, the visions that passed through his head were of terracotta warriors and Nemesai and a long, vicious battle that had occurred here, in this subterranean city, the final resting place of emperors and artisans and beggars and soldiers. He wanted to shift the red dreams to something more mercurial. He wanted to somehow help in his last moments. The weight of liquid metal crushed him, enveloped him, invaded his body...but it had been too much, too quickly, and never had time to infuse with him.

That was Keith's final understanding.

His final thought, however, was of Christine.

Under the quicksilver surface, he smiled one last time before dying.

6

"Where is he?" Christine peered into the silver depths. "Do you see him? Did he surface?"

Before Atiya could respond, their radios crackled. A man shouted at them in Chinese. Although she couldn't understand his words, Atiya recognized his demeanor. She turned back to Christine.

"I think the cavalry just arrived."

Christine responded, but Atiya couldn't hear her, because the footsteps below had grown to a crescendo.

7

The girl and her grandfather watched the soldiers go into the earth. They sat, made a campfire, and cooked rice, watching as no one reemerged from the tomb.

They heard thunder under the earth, but no screams, and no shouts of victory.

A calm settled over them, and the tomb, as if all the elements of the world waited.

8

The Nemesai rose from the shadows.

JOHN URBANCIK is a writer, photographer, poet, and adventurer whose books include the *DarkWalker* series, the *InkStains* series, *The Corpse and the Girl from Miami*, *Stale Reality*, *John the Revelator*, and many more. Although he is never in one place for long, he currently resides in Florida.

BRIAN KEENE is a best-selling writer and podcaster whose books include *The Rising* series, *The Lost Level* series, *Ghoul*, *The Complex*, *End of the Road*, and many more. He lives along the banks of the Susquehanna River in rural Pennsylvania.